Just Mommy
and Me

This book is dedicated to my husband, Gino,
and my two beloved children,
Ilyse April and Ilijah A.
—T.J.M.

For my son, Eric,
who was my little monkey.
—K.B.

Just Mommy and Me
Text copyright © 2004 by Tara Jaye Morrow
Illustrations copyright © 2004 by Katy Bratun
Printed in Mexico. All rights reserved.
www.harperchildrens.com

Library of Congress Cataloging-in-Publication Data
Morrow, Tara Jaye.
   Just Mommy and me / by Tara Jaye Morrow ; illustrated by
Katy Bratun.
       p.   cm.
   Summary: A monkey mother and child spend a wonderful
day together, from morning bananas to sleeping under the
moon.
   ISBN 0-06-000724-9 ISBN 0-06-000725-7 (lib. bdg.)
   [1. Mother and child—Fiction.   2. Monkeys—Fiction.
3. Stories in rhyme.] I. Bratun, Katy, ill. II. Title.
PZ8.3.C343 Ju 2004   2002001469
[E]—dc21   CIP
                                                 AC

Typography by Elynn Cohen 1 2 3 4 5 6 7 8 9 10 ❖
First Edition

Just Mommy and Me

by Tara Jaye Morrow • illustrated by Katy Bratun

HarperCollins*Publishers*

If I were a monkey who swung on a tree

and you were my mommy, who swung after me,

and we ate bananas until there were none

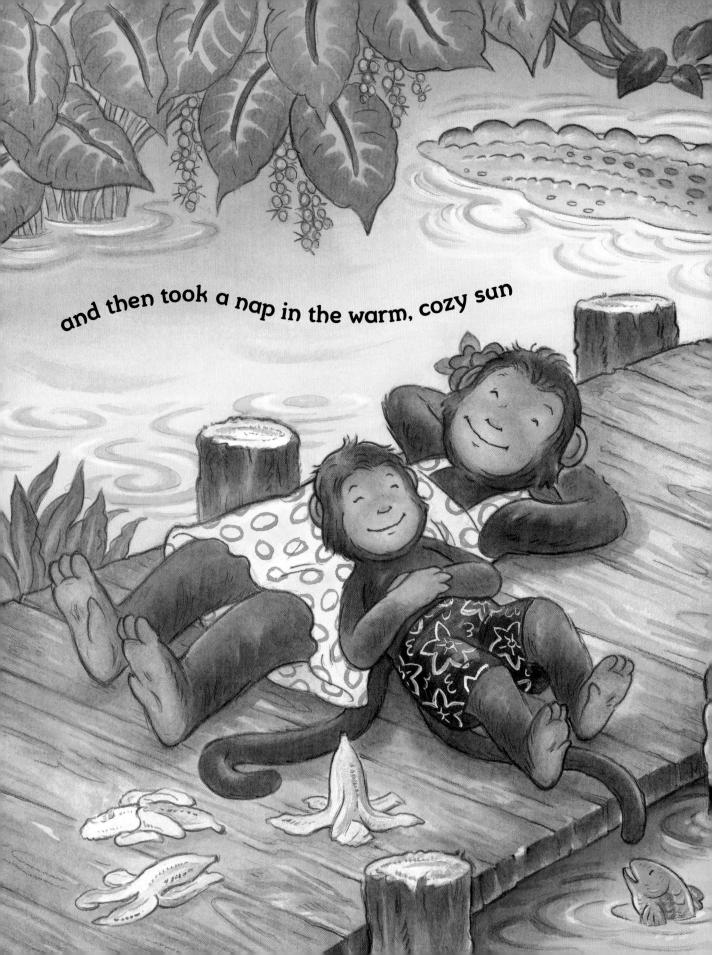

and then took a nap in the warm, cozy sun

and when we woke up, sang our favorite song

while clapping and jumping and dancing along . . .

If we were two monkeys who played hide-and-seek
and I promised you, Mommy, that I wouldn't peek

and we took a walk in a cool, shady place

and saw who could make the silliest face

and we picked some flowers to put in your hat,
and I got to choose them—you know I'd love that!

If we were two monkeys just having a ball,

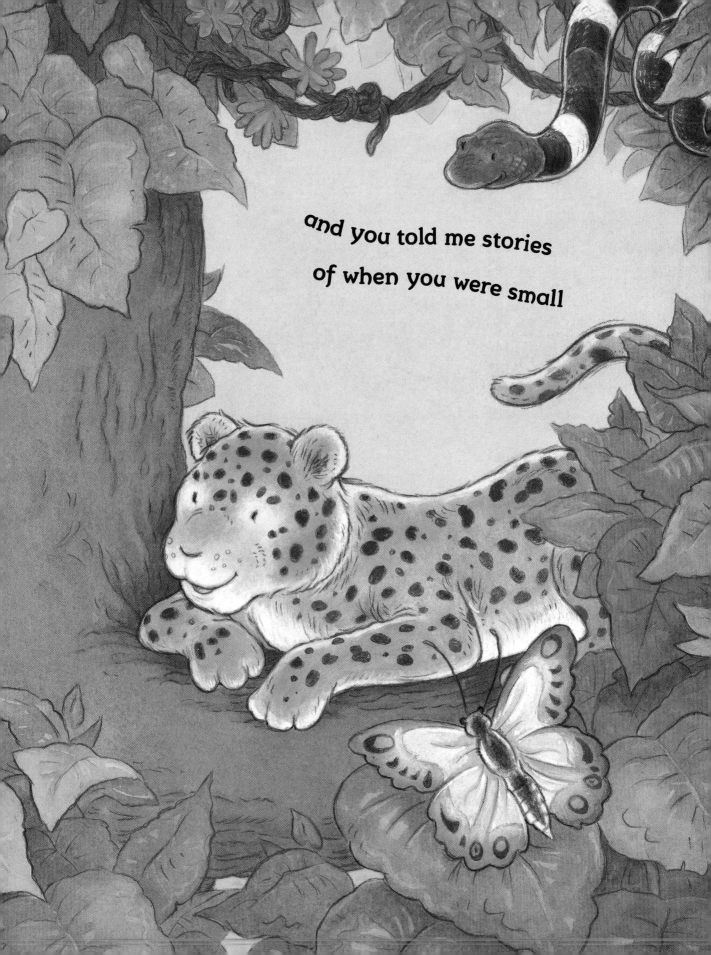

and you told me stories
of when you were small

and we took a swim with the fishies and frogs
and splashed in the water and rolled on the logs

and snuggled up close while we looked at the skies

to watch the sun set and the stars wink their eyes . . .

If we did these things
all the day long, and soon,
we both fell asleep under
bright Mr. Moon . . .

imagine how happy
and fun it would be,
if we were two monkeys,
just Mommy and me!